LITTLE PANDA

Piers Harper

MACMILLAN CHILDREN'S BOOKS

"Little Panda, you're home at last."
Little Panda looked up happily and snuggled up to mummy panda.
"And this is the best home ever," he yawned.

That's just what he did. He spotted the most
wonderful place to sleep right in front of his nose.
It was safe, snugly and perfect. He ran as fast
as he could towards it. Then a familiar
voice whispered . . .

Climbing into the swaying branches was difficult,
and the tree began to lean and bow.

"Your home is much too high," wailed Little Panda.
"I think I should look for somewhere to sleep that's
closer to the ground."

By now, Little Panda was feeling very sleepy indeed. It was getting dark and soon the stars would be out. Little Panda wondered if he would ever find a comfortable place to sleep when he saw a face in the trees up ahead.

"Why are you out so late, Little Panda?" asked Red Panda.

"I'm looking for a place to sleep," yawned Little Panda.

"Then climb up here with me," said Red Panda. "There's plenty of room for two."

The sticks and twigs stuck into Little Panda's fur and, because Little Panda was heavier than Crane, the nest began to sink into the swamp.

"Whoops!" cried Little Panda. "Thank you, Crane, but your home is too uncomfortable for me."

At last, Little Panda noticed a crane sitting on a nest of downy white feathers. It looked like the most comfortable place in the world, and Little Panda was feeling very sleepy.

"Climb in," smiled Crane, so Little Panda clambered in and settled down.

Soon the monkeys were all talking at once, chattering into Little Panda's ear, and the baby monkeys loved climbing on Little Panda's back. Little Panda's head felt sore from all the noise.

"Thank you for letting me stay," he said. "But your home is too noisy for me."

As Little Panda padded deeper into the forest,
he could hear a chattering noise up above him.
The trees were full of golden monkeys.
"Hello, Little Panda!" they said. "What are you doing
so deep in the forest?"
When Little Panda explained that he was looking for
somewhere to sleep, the kind monkeys invited him to sleep
in the branches.

"What are you doing in my den?" growled Tiger, swishing his stripy tail. "You can't sleep here."

Little Panda looked at Tiger's sharp teeth.

"You're right," he said. "Your home is much too dark and scary for me."

So Little Panda ran away as fast as he could.

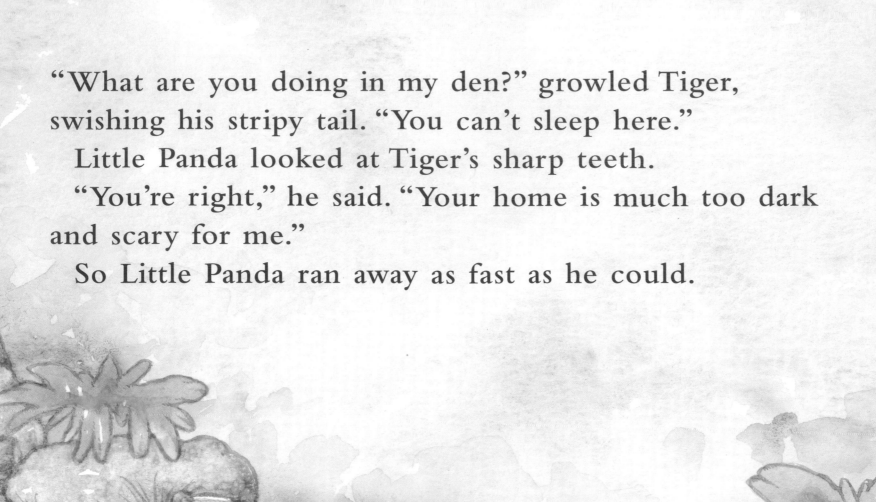

Little Panda padded on through the forest, looking for somewhere to sleep. Soon, he came to a cave.

"This looks perfect," he thought. But, once inside, Little Panda began to feel scared. It was dark and full of strange noises, and what was that big shadow on the wall?

Before long, though, Little Panda began to yawn.

"This looks like a good place for a nap," he thought, as he wriggled inside a hollow log. But something prickly soon blocked his way.

"This is my home," snuffled Porcupine. "But you can stay for a while."

"Ouch! No, thank you," said Little Panda. "Your home is too prickly for me."

Little Panda had been playing in the morning sun and now it was time for his nap.

"Time to settle down, Little Panda," said his mother gently. But Little Panda didn't feel at all sleepy. There were too many exciting things to see and do in the forest, so he ran off to explore.

For Daniel, Nicholas and Sadie

First published in 2005 by Macmillan Children's Books
a division of Macmillan Publishers Limited
20 New Wharf Road, London N1 9RR
Basingstoke and Oxford
Associated companies worldwide
www.panmacmillan.com

Produced by Fernleigh Books
1A London Road, Enfield
Middlesex EN2 6BN

Text copyright © 2005 Fernleigh Books
Illustrations copyright © 2005 Piers Harper

ISBN 1 405 02173 X

1 3 5 7 9 8 6 4 2

A CIP catalogue record for this book is available
form the British Library.

Manufactured in China.